SACRAMENTO PUBLIC LIBRARY

D0382228

DAREDEVIL DUCK

Charlie Alder

RP | KIDS

PHILADELPHIA · LONDON

Also starring:

Jonathan, Coffee Support Team and Daredevil Dad

Marlo, Teresa, and Running Press, for their unwavering support, encouraging words, and handholding

Vicki and the Bright team, Stardust Sprinklers, every one of them

Annabel and Katy, for beachside brainstorming

Kirsten, for loud cheering from the front row

Copyright © 2015 by Charlie Alder

All rights reserved under the Pan-American and International Copyright Conventions

Printed in China

This book may not be reproduced in whole or in part, in any form or by any means, electronic or mechanical, including photocopying, recording, or by any information storage and retrieval system now known or hereafter invented, without written permission from the publisher.

Books published by Running Press are available at special discounts for bulk purchases in the United States by corporations, institutions, and other organizations. For more information, please contact the Special Markets Department at the Perseus Books Group, 2300 Chestnut Street, Suite 200, Philadelphia, PA 19103, or call (800) 810-4145, ext. 5000, or e-mail special.markets@perseusbooks.com.

ISBN 978-0-7624-5456-3
Library of Congress Control Number: 2014951327

9 8 7 6 5 4 3 2 1
Digit on the right indicates the number of this printing

Designed by T.L. Bonaddio
Edited by Marlo Scrimizzi
Typography: ITC Century

Published by Running Press Kids
An Imprint of Running Press Book Publishers
A Member of the Perseus Books Group
2300 Chestnut Street
Philadelphia, PA 19103–4371

Visit us on the web!
www.runningpress.com/rpkids

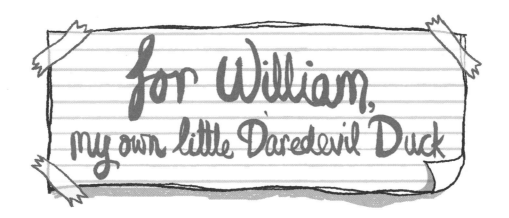

HERO
HELMET
(EXTRA
STRONG)

D.D.

X-RAY
GLASSES

SUPER
HERO
CAPE

SUPER
SPEEDY
(SLIGHTLY
SQUEAKY)
TRICYCLE

He is the
bravest duck
in the
whole world.

(Well, kind of.)

Oh, there you are!
Come on out.

Er . . .
Daredevil Duck?
Where did you go?
Hellooooo?

You see, Daredevil Duck *wants* to be brave.

But sometimes he's not.

He is afraid of things
that are too dark,

things that are
too fluttery,

things that are
too wet,

and he is
positively
terrified
of things
that are
too high.

Sometimes, the other ducks tease him.

And when they do, their words can hurt.

One day,

Daredevil

Duck was

floating on his Daredevil Rubber Ring, dreaming

of being BRAVE.

Daredevil Duck was so frightened.

SPLASH!

When he reached the end of the lake,
he ran to his Super Speedy (slightly squeaky) tricycle.
He peddled as fast as his little legs could take him.

He peddled through the dark woods *(as spoooooky as can be)*,

beneath the fluttery leaves *(always swirling and twirling)*,

through the deep puddles *(the wettest ones you could find)*,

and up and over the hills *(that were so very high)*.

But somewhere along his travels
Daredevil Duck got a little confused.

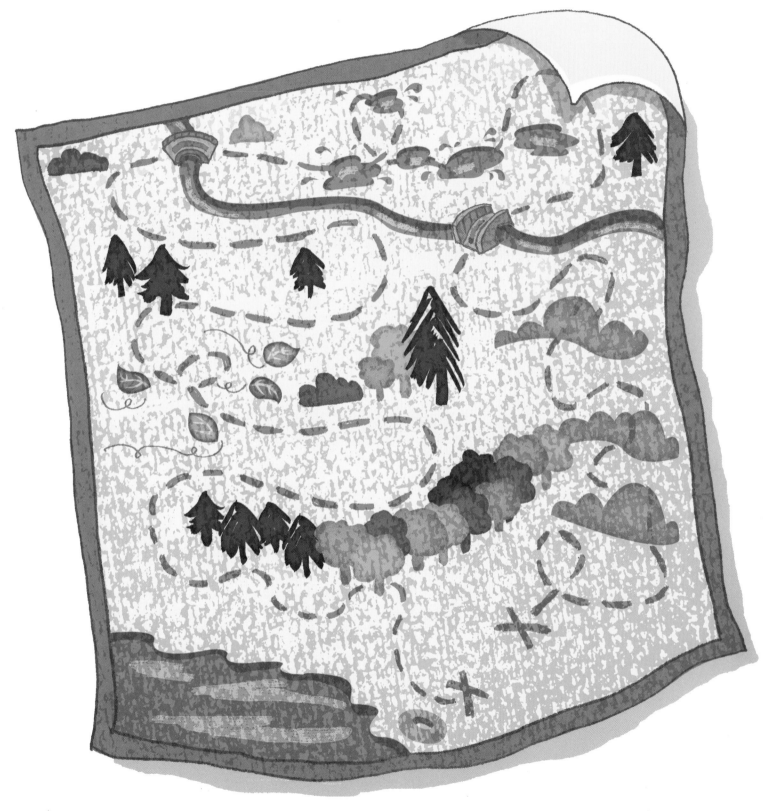

He ended up right where he started.

"Hello again!" said the chatty mole. "Can you help me, please? My balloon is stuck in that tree!"

Slowly, Daredevil Duck climbed up the tree.

. . . JUMPED!

Daredevil Duck couldn't believe
it. He rescued the balloon!

started   to

And then the breeze

higher . . .   and higher . . .

take him away · · ·

Daredevil Duck looked around.
The fluffy clouds were so close
he could almost touch them.

He started to feel happy . . .

When the wind stopped,
Daredevil Duck clung to the yellow balloon.
The little mole was scampering toward him.

Daredevil Duck started to feel scared again . . .

. . . until he noticed the mole's big smile.

"Wow, thanks, little duck!
You must be the bravest duck
in the whole world!" said the mole.

This time, Daredevil Duck believed him.

From that day on, Daredevil Duck
tried to be brave
in lots of different ways . . .

**he roller-skated
(with friends),**

**he rolled
*(down many
many hills)*,**

he tried zooming
(without holding on!),

he jumped *(quite)* high,

and he even turned
off the light after
getting into bed.

And whenever the other
ducks start to laugh
at Daredevil Duck, he
reminds them of
Yellow Balloon Day.

And that he really, truly, absolutely is . . .

(Well, most of the time.)